The Usborne
First
Encyclopedia
of
Animals

Written by
Paul Dowswell

Designed by
Karen Tomlins and
Verinder Bhachu

Digital colouring: Fiona Johnson
Cover design: Mary Cartwright
Managing editor: Judy Tatchell
Consultant: Margaret Rostron

Contents

Animal world

There are millions of different animals, but they all fall into groups which have features in common. Here are five groups which this book looks at in detail.

A bird's shape helps it move fast through the air.

Mammals

Mammals feed milk to their babies. Almost all have hair or fur, and most are lively and curious. From polar bears to camels, mammals can be found all over the world.

Birds

Birds are the only animals that have feathers. They all have wings, but not all of them can fly. Some are powerful runners or swimmers. All birds lay eggs, and take care of their babies.

These lion cubs, like all baby mammals, are looked after by their mother.

Reptiles

Reptiles have dry, scaly skin and almost all lay eggs. Although you can find reptiles in most countries, they mainly live in the warmer parts of the world.

This is a chameleon. It can change colour to match its surroundings.

Creepy-crawlies

The world is teeming with creepy-crawlies such as insects, spiders and centipedes. They make up four-fifths of all known animal types.

The most common type of creepy-crawlies are insects. They all have six legs, and most have wings.

Creepy-crawlies come in all sorts of shapes. This long, wriggly one is a centipede.

Like most insects, this wasp can fly.

Water life

Many different animals live in water – from fish to mammals such as dolphins and seals, and creatures such as jellyfish and lobsters. Some animals are even able to live in the deepest ocean.

Like all fish, a lionfish is able to breathe under water.

Mammals

The animals on these two pages look different, but whether they swim in the sea, fly in the air, or live on land, they are all mammals. There are thousands of different kinds of mammals, including you – humans are mammals, too.

Chimpanzees live in the forests of Africa.

Keeping warm

A mammal's body makes its own warmth and its temperature stays the same whether the day is hot or cold. This is called being warm-blooded. Mammals use a lot of energy keeping warm, and need to eat frequently.

The fur on this chimp helps to keep its body warm when its surroundings are cold.

Food for baby

All mammal mothers feed their babies milk. This is produced by glands, called mammary glands, on the mother's chest or belly. Milk is a rich source of food, and is easy for a baby to swallow.

This baby deer is drinking milk which is made inside its mother's body.

Flying mammal

Bats are the only mammals that can fly. They use their arms as wings. Each wing is made of skin, which stretches over the bones of the arms and fingers.

Fruit bat

Here you can see how a bat uses its arm as a wing. Long fingers support the wing skin.

Swimmers

Some mammals, such as whales, dolphins and seals, live in the sea. Like all mammals, they breathe air, so they need to come to the surface regularly.

Whales are the biggest animals in the world.

Unlike most mammals, whales do not have hair on their bodies.

Egg layers

Only three kinds of mammals lay eggs, rather than give birth. One is the duck-billed platypus. It lays its eggs in a nest in a riverbank burrow. When the babies hatch, they lick milk which oozes from their mother's skin.

Duck-billed platypus

What's for dinner?

Some animals eat plants, some eat meat, and some eat both. Plant-eaters have flat teeth to help them chew their food. Meat-eaters have sharp teeth to kill and eat their food.

A gerenuk reaching for a leaf

Plant food

Many plant-eaters eat only one sort of plant, or just one part of a plant. Because of this, different plant-eaters can live in the same area and all have enough food. Here is an example of this, in the African grassland.

Zebras graze on the grass.

Rhinos nibble at the bushes.

Giraffes eat tree-top leaves.

Gnawing teeth

Rat

Rats eat almost anything and can even gnaw through metal. They are a type of mammal called a rodent. All rodents have strong front teeth which never stop growing, and are worn down when they eat.

Bamboo eater

Living on only one sort of food can be risky. A giant panda eats huge amounts of bamboo. In some years the bamboo grows poorly, and many pandas starve.

Pandas are also able to eat birds and rodents, but they do not do this very often.

This panda is eating a bamboo shoot.

Meat-eater

Meat gives an animal more energy than plants, so meat-eaters, such as this lioness, spend less time eating than plant-eaters.

A lioness's jaws are packed with powerful muscles to help her kill and eat her prey.

Chaser

All big cats creep up on their prey, then rush out and grab it. Cheetahs do this too, but are also able to chase their victims over long distances. The chase makes them tired, but the meat they eat gives them back their energy.

A cheetah running at full speed. It can run at 115kmph (70mph).

The lioness has different-shaped teeth to let her grip, tear and slice her food.

9

Night mammals

Huge numbers of animals, including half of all types of mammals, come out at night. Many are meat-eaters that feed on other night animals.

This tarsier is out hunting. It eats insects, lizards, and even small bats.

Night sight

Many animals that hunt at night have good eyesight to help them find food.

Some have a special layer at the back of their eyes called a tapetum. This helps them pick up every little glimmer of light so they can see better in the dark.

You can see the tapetum glowing at the back of an animal's eye, if it is caught in a bright light.

Notice how big the tarsier's eyes are compared with its body.

Night animals usually have bigger eyes than day animals. Big eyes pick up much more light.

Ears and echoes

Most night animals have good hearing and big ears. This helps them pick up any noise which may lead them to food.

Bats hunt at night, and squeak as they fly. The sound of the squeak bounces off other animals, and comes back to the bat as an echo. The echo tells the bat where the animal is.

A bat sends out squeaks as it flies around.

The sound bounces off a nearby insect as an echo.

A leaf-nosed bat hunting at night

The bat's big ears help it pick up every little sound.

Unusually for night animals, bats have small eyes and poor eyesight. Their hearing makes up for this.

Cool time

A lot of desert animals only come out in the cool of the night. It is too hot to hunt in the day.

This kangaroo rat comes out of its den when the sun goes down.

Food sniffer

Badgers have poor eyesight, but their sense of smell is superb. They have good hearing too.

Badgers sniff on the ground for food with their sensitive noses.

Hide and seek

Many animals have colours and patterns on their bodies to help them blend in with their surroundings. This is called camouflage. It can help them hunt other creatures without being seen. Camouflage also makes it easier for animals to hide from their enemies.

Stripes and spots

A lot of mammals that live in jungles or forests have stripes or spots on their fur. These match the patterns made by sunlight as it streams down through the trees.

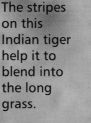

The stripes on this Indian tiger help it to blend into the long grass.

Most animals see in black and white, so this leopard in a tree is hard for them to see.

Plain coats

Dull colours can also provide camouflage. These gazelles blend in with dry, brown grassland.

Gazelles leap high in the air to show enemies they are difficult to catch.

Gazelles' pale bellies and darker backs make them harder to see from a distance in the grassland.

Green fur

This three-toed sloth lives in the rainforest. Its grey fur is covered in tiny green plants. These colours help it hide from its enemies among the leaves.

Three-toed sloth

Hazy stripes

Zebras have a strong pattern on their coats. But from a distance, the hazy heat on the African plains blurs the zebra's shape, and the stripes make it harder to see.

All change

By changing colour with the seasons, animals such as mountain hares and arctic foxes stay camouflaged. Their fur is white in winter, but brown in summer, to match the plants and rocks.

A mountain hare's white coat matches the winter snow.

An arctic fox during the winter

An arctic fox during the summer

Escaping from enemies

Only the strongest, fiercest and biggest animals have no fear of being attacked by enemies. Most animals in the wild live in constant danger of being eaten. Here you can see some of the ways in which they protect themselves.

A squirrel has sharp claws to help it grip branches on the trees it climbs.

Up and away

Running away is often the best defence. Squirrels escape by climbing trees. They can leap onto very thin branches where their enemies cannot follow.

This grey squirrel is on the lookout for enemies. It is very nimble, and can quickly shoot up a tree to safety.

Spikes for protection

The sharp spines on the back of a spiny anteater help protect it from enemies. Below you can see one of the ways in which it defends itself.

If an anteater is threatened, it begins to dig down.

It burrows down into the earth using its long claws.

Spines will cut the enemy's paws if it tries to dig it out.

A nasty smell

If a skunk is threatened, it turns its tail towards the enemy. It has a gland there which can squirt out a smelly liquid. The stink is so horrible that most enemies will leave it alone.

A skunk raises its tail when it is ready to squirt.

This is an addax. Its horns get bigger as it grows older.

Horned beasts

Some plant-eating animals have sharp horns on their head. Many use these to protect themselves from meat-eating enemies. The males also use the horns in fights with other males when they are competing to mate with females.

Horns are made of bone, with an outer layer of hard, fingernail-like tissue.

Scaly armour

Armadillos have horny, tough plates which protect them like a suit of armour. The plates stretch from the tip of their nose to the end of their tail. Each plate is linked to the next, so the armadillo is completely protected.

When an armadillo is attacked, it rolls into a tight ball.

15

Living together

Many mammals live in groups, rather than by themselves. This is because living in a group is safer, even for fierce hunters.

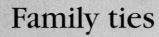

Prairie dogs live in groups in the grasslands of North America.

Zebra groups

Zebras live in small family groups made up of a male, several females, and their young. The group stays together as part of a larger herd.

Zebras in the same family nuzzle each other.

Family ties

Prairie dogs live in burrows in large family groups. When they meet, they sniff each other, like the two shown above.

The smell tells one prairie dog whether the other is a member of its family.

These zebras are part of a large herd. There may be several hundred zebras in a herd.

The zebras below are looking out for enemies while the rest of the herd feed.

Life with the lions

Lions are the only cats that live in groups. They survive by working closely with each other.

The male lions guard the group's territory. The lionesses hunt in small teams, setting up ambushes and diversions. They also look after the cubs.

A group of lions is called a pride.

Swingers

Gibbons live in families. A male and female mate for life and have a baby every two or three years.

The young stay with their parents for up to six years. Each family member searches for food on its own but they keep in touch in the dense jungle by calling to each other.

A pair of gibbons

Baby mammals

Most baby mammals are helpless when they are born, and need a lot of care. Animals that can hide their young in a safe place, such as a nest, usually have several babies. Animals that cannot do this usually have only one or two babies at a time, so they can guard them carefully.

Giraffe calf

Giraffes usually have one baby at a time. A baby giraffe is an easy target for a lion, so its mother must protect it. If her baby is threatened, she can deliver a deadly kick with her powerful legs.

Large litters

Mice have large litters – eight babies is quite usual. The babies are born in a nest which keeps them warm. Many young are still caught by enemies such as owls and cats.

This giraffe mother licks her baby to clean it, so its scent does not attract an enemy.

Baby mice stay with their mother for less than a month.

Learning what to do

Polar bear cubs spend between two and three years with their mothers, learning how to survive in the Arctic. The mother teaches her baby how to hunt for food. The cubs leave their mother when they are old enough to hunt successfully on their own.

Baby polar bears stay close to their mothers.

Pouch home

Marsupial mammals, like this kangaroo, carry their babies around in a built-in pouch. The baby feeds on milk from a nipple inside the pouch. It also goes into the pouch if it is frightened, or needs to rest.

A baby kangaroo can travel this way until it is a year old.

Long childhood

Elephants look after their babies longer than any other animals except humans. A young elephant will be cared for by its mother for up to ten years. They live in family groups so a baby is also watched over by its aunties.

This baby elephant is learning to use its trunk to drink and bathe.

Sea mammals

Some mammals spend all their lives at sea. Others live near the shore, and spend some of the time on the beach.

A life at sea

There are three types of mammals that never come ashore – dolphins, whales and sea cows. All of these animals have flippers and a tail fin.

Whales

Whales are the biggest animals on Earth. They have a layer of fat under their skin called blubber, to help keep them warm.

This huge humpback whale can be found in seas throughout the world.

A whale breathes through a blow-hole in its head. Stale air is blown out with a noisy snort.

Sea grazer

The animal on the right is called a sea cow, because it grazes on sea grasses and other underwater plants. It has a split upper lip to help it grasp its food.

Sea cows are gentle, placid creatures.

20

In and out

Seals, sea lions and walruses are sea mammals that spend part of their lives on land. They have flipper-like back legs, instead of a tail fin.

Seals are brilliant swimmers, but clumsy on land.

Life on land

The main reason seals, sea lions and walruses come out of the sea is to mate and give birth. Below you can see how a ringed seal makes a den for its baby in the snow.

This female seal is looking for a gap in the ice. She will squeeze through to the snow above and begin to make her den.

She makes a hollow in the dense snow. When she has finished, her baby will have a safe and cosy shelter.

The baby seal, called a pup, spends six weeks in the den.

Dolphins

Dolphins are clever and friendly animals. They are also very fast swimmers. Like whales and sea cows, they wave their tail fins up and down to push themselves through the water.

These are Atlantic spotted dolphins. Like all dolphins, they prefer to travel around in groups.

Bird life

Birds are found almost everywhere in the world. They are the only animals to have feathers. Not all of them fly, but those that cannot are usually superb swimmers or runners.

Fit for flying

Many birds are brilliant fliers. Most of their bones are hollow, so they are light. Strong chest muscles power their wings. The sleek shape of their bodies helps them move quickly through the air.

This goose is coming in to land. Its feet are lowered, ready to meet the ground. Its wings are spread out, to slow it down.

Body shapes

Birds have different body shapes, depending on their way of life. A goose's strong, muscle-packed body is ideal for the long flights it makes, when it travels to warmer countries for the winter. A kingfisher's small, arrow-like body lets it dart in and out of the water as it hunts for fish.

The kingfisher has a long, sharp beak, which it uses to spear fish.

22

Types of feathers

Feathers keep birds warm, help them fly, and give them colour. They have three kinds. Fluffy down feathers keep them warm. Short, sturdy body feathers keep them dry. Long flight feathers help them to take off, fly and land.

You can see the flight feathers of this eagle on its wing.

Migration

Half of all types of birds fly long distances, moving from one feeding or breeding site to another. This is called migration. Birds are the greatest travellers in the animal world.

In winter, these geese fly from Canada to Mexico in search of food.

Fluffy feathers

Baby birds are covered in warm down feathers. They grow body and flight feathers when they are older.

This baby bird has a down coat to keep it warm in its cliff top nest.

Feather care

All birds get dirty and untidy. They have to clean and smooth down their feathers with their beak, to keep them working properly.

This heron is cleaning its feathers.

Colours

Birds have all sorts of colours. Some have dull colours to help them hide in their surroundings. Others have bright, vivid colours to help other birds recognize them.

Pretty pink

Flamingos get their colour from the pink shrimps and other small animals that they eat. If they did not eat this food, they would be a dull yellowy-brown.

A flamingo bending to feed in the water

Bright birds

Most parrots are beautiful colours. Their luminous feathers stand out against the green forests where they live, and help other parrots find them.

This red-capped parrot lives in the forests of Western Australia.

24

Attracting females

Many male birds have bright colours to help them attract a mate. Females, in contrast, often look much duller.

These two brightly-coloured male pheasants use their vivid feathers to try to impress a female.

Lady Amherst's pheasant (male)

Chinese monal pheasant (male)

Bright bills

When it is time to mate, male and female tufted puffins grow colourful feathers at the back of their head.

Their beaks also become much brighter and grow an extra layer. When the breeding season is over, the new layer drops off.

Before puffins mate, they rub their bright beaks together.

Ptarmigan

Hiding away

Many birds have colours which help them hide from their enemies. In winter, a ptarmigan has white feathers to match the snow. When the snow melts, the feathers turn browner, to match the surroundings. Most baby birds have dull-coloured feathers, too.

Almost all baby birds have camouflage colours to keep them hidden from hunters.

In the air

All birds have wings, even those which cannot fly. Being able to fly lets a bird catch food in the air, or travel to warmer places to build a nest and find food. Flying also helps birds to escape from their enemies.

Taking off

Not all birds take off in the same way. Small birds can just jump into the air, but large birds, such as swans, have to work a lot harder to get airborne.

A swan stretches out its wings.

It flaps and runs along the water.

It launches itself into the air.

A stork stretches into a streamlined shape to fly through the air. This one is carrying branches for its nest.

Big and small flyers

Small birds beat their wings quickly to stay in the air. Most have short wings which are ideal for flitting through trees and branches. Most big birds have large wings. They glide to save energy, only beating their wings now and then.

Because birds have hollow bones, even big ones are usually light enough to fly.

When a tiny hummingbird beats its wings very fast, it can hover in the air.

Birds that cannot fly

Ostriches are the biggest birds in the world. They are too heavy for their little wings to carry them into the air. Instead, they have huge, powerful legs and run very fast.

Ostriches running

Penguins cannot fly, but they can swim underwater, and use their wings like flippers. They are very graceful swimmers, and move very quickly.

Penguins dive under water to hunt for fish.

Bodies and beaks

The shape of a bird's body and beak helps it to both find and eat the kind of food it likes. You can see here that there are huge differences in body and beak shapes.

Sea life

Puffins live by the sea and hunt fish. Their stubby, muscular bodies and short wings help them swim well underwater. They can fly, but they are much clumsier in the air than in the sea.

Wings and claws

This bald eagle's huge wings let it glide effortlessly over water as it searches for fish. Its sharp claws hold the prey tightly as it returns to its nest to feed.

This bald eagle has sharp claws for grasping fish.

This is a puffin. Its webbed feet help it paddle in the sea.

Beak shapes

Birds use their beaks as tools to help them find food. This toucan's long beak lets it reach for fruit among dense forest branches.

The toucan's jagged beak helps it to grip fruit firmly.

Diggers

Like many river and seashore birds, the scarlet ibis has a long, thin beak. It uses it to poke around for little shrimps and worms at the muddy edges of rivers.

Scarlet ibis

Spears and nets

Many birds eat other animals. Some are fierce hunters who can kill prey as big as a monkey. Here are three flesh-eating birds who use their beaks in different ways.

A heron uses its dagger-like beak to spear fish.

A vulture has a hooked beak. This lets it tear meat from a dead animal.

A pelican uses its sack-shaped beak like a fishing net.

Bird messages

Birds pass messages to each other by squawking and singing, but this is not the only way they "talk" to each other. Their body language also lets other birds know what they intend to do.

Birdsong

All birds make calls, but some birds, known as songbirds, sing more complex tunes. Usually the males sing to attract a mate, or show they own a certain territory.

A meadowlark sings as he patrols his territory, warning other birds not to trespass.

Dancing

Many male birds, such as the booby on the right, dance to attract a female. If the booby succeeds, the female will come and touch his neck with her beak. The grebes below are also performing a courtship dance.

A grebe goes to another with wings arched.

They waggle their heads at each other.

They offer each other weeds.

This male booby is trying to attract a female by lifting his bright blue feet high in the air.

Showing off

Another way of attracting a mate is to show astonishing colours. A prairie chicken blows up big yellow air sacs either side of its neck. A tragopan puffs up its chest to show bright red and blue flaps of skin.

A male tragopan, showing off

Here you can see one of the male prairie chicken's yellow air sacs.

Love nest

Male bower birds make a little hollow in the grass, and decorate it with objects such as shells, feathers, and buttons. When females visit, the bower bird picks up one of these objects and struts around with it.

The male bower bird (blue) is trying to attract a female.

Watch out!

Birds use signals to threaten rivals. Letting other birds know they are angry is usually enough to scare them off, and avoid a fight. The Philippine eagle on the right is warning a rival that it is ready to attack.

The eagle raises feathers on its head to frighten rivals.

Nests and chicks

Soon after a female bird has mated, she lays her eggs. She needs to sit on them to keep them warm, or the babies inside will die.

A safe spot

Most birds build nests to protect the mother and her eggs from enemies. Nests also make a safe place for the babies when they hatch.

Types of nest

Each type of bird has its own way of building a nest, but most nests have similar features. Many are cup-shaped, and made of mud, hair, feathers and twigs. Below you can see three different types.

A swallow's nest is made of mud and stuck to a wall.

A tailor bird sews big leaves together with plant fibres.

A long-tailed tit makes a nest of moss, lichen and cobwebs.

This Eurasian tit's nest is made of twigs and reed fibres. It is hanging from a tree branch.

Breaking out

Birds sit on their eggs for two weeks or more. (Bigger birds sit for longer.) When the baby is ready to hatch, it chips its way out of the egg. Most bird babies need a lot of looking after.

This baby moorhen is chipping its way out of its egg.

A hoopoe feeding a hungry chick

Hungry babies

All baby birds are extremely hungry, and need a constant supply of food. The hoopoe, above, makes hundreds of journeys to and from its nest every day. It brings termites, caterpillars and other insects to feed its three or four chicks.

Protecting the family

This mother swan and her babies (called cygnets) are gathered around their nest. Cygnets spend around four months with their parents, who protect them and take them to feeding grounds.

When the babies leave the nest they live alone, but pair up with a mate when they are two years old.

Swans build a large waterside nest from plant stalks.

Snap and grab

Most reptiles are meat-eaters. They often catch their prey in extraordinary ways.

Shooter

A chameleon eats insects. When it gets near to its prey, it wraps its tail around a branch. Then it takes careful aim and shoots out its long, sticky tongue. It needs to be silent, fast and accurate, because insects move so fast.

Nasty surprise

Crocodiles lurk just below the surface of a river. They spring out and catch an animal drinking at the water's edge. A crocodile cannot chew, so it swallows small prey whole. It uses its powerful jaws to bite and crush larger prey before it swallows them.

This chameleon is ready to strike. It stays very still, so the insect does not notice it. Only its eyes move.

It shoots out its tongue, which is curled up in its mouth. Its tongue is nearly as long as its body.

The insect sticks to the tongue. It is pulled in and eaten.

This baby crocodile has caught a frog in its teeth. It will flip back its head and toss the frog into its mouth.

Frogs are one of a baby crocodile's favourite meals.

Snake table manners

Snakes have several fascinating and revolting ways of killing their food. Many can eat animals which are much bigger than themselves.

A snake can separate its upper and lower jaws. This lets it open its mouth very wide. Its body also stretches to hold the food it is eating.

The boomslang snake climbs trees and snatches birds from their nests.

Like many snakes, the coral snake has poisonous fangs. These paralyse its prey.

This anaconda has squeezed a crocodile to death.

A flap of skin covers the back of the crocodile's throat, to stop it swallowing water when it dives.

You can see how the snake's jaws separate, so it can swallow this huge meal.

Breaking out

Birds sit on their eggs for two weeks or more. (Bigger birds sit for longer.) When the baby is ready to hatch, it chips its way out of the egg. Most bird babies need a lot of looking after.

This baby moorhen is chipping its way out of its egg.

A hoopoe feeding a hungry chick

Hungry babies

All baby birds are extremely hungry, and need a constant supply of food. The hoopoe, above, makes hundreds of journeys to and from its nest every day. It brings termites, caterpillars and other insects to feed its three or four chicks.

Protecting the family

This mother swan and her babies (called cygnets) are gathered around their nest. Cygnets spend around four months with their parents, who protect them and take them to feeding grounds.

When the babies leave the nest they live alone, but pair up with a mate when they are two years old.

Swans build a large waterside nest from plant stalks.

Reptile life

What makes a reptile a reptile? It has scaly skin, it lays eggs and it is "cold-blooded". This means its body does not make heat and is as warm or as cold as its surroundings. Lizards, snakes, turtles and crocodiles are all reptiles.

This snake is a tree python. It hunts birds.

Snakes

All snakes are meat-eaters. Some eat insects and worms. Some can eat prey as big as a crocodile. You can find snakes all over the world, except in Antarctica.

Lizards

Most lizards are small, nimble creatures, although a few can grow to be as much as 3m (10ft) long. Like snakes, they can be found almost everywhere on Earth.

Crocodiles

Crocodiles, and their close relatives, alligators, are fierce hunters. They can be found on river banks in hot countries. In the right conditions, crocodiles can live for over 100 years.

This calotes lizard lives in the forests of Southern India.

The long tail helps the calotes balance on thin branches.

Nile crocodile

Turtles

Turtles spend their lives in warm, shallow seas, and only ever come onto land to lay eggs. Some swim hundreds of miles to find a place to have babies.

Turtles have flippers instead of legs.

Hawksbill turtle

Tortoises

Tortoises are similar to turtles, but they live on land instead of water.

Tortoises are well protected by their hard outer shells.

Hot and cold

As reptiles are cold-blooded, heat and cold affect them more than warm-blooded animals. If they are too cold, they become sluggish. If they are too hot, they dry up and die. A reptile spends a lot of the day trying to stay at the right temperature.

This iguana's leathery skin helps prevent it from drying up.

Morning. Bask in sun to warm up after cool night.

Noon. Hide in shade at hottest time of day.

Afternoon. Move in and out of sun, to keep warm or cool.

Snap and grab

Most reptiles are meat-eaters. They often catch their prey in extraordinary ways.

Shooter

A chameleon eats insects. When it gets near to its prey, it wraps its tail around a branch. Then it takes careful aim and shoots out its long, sticky tongue. It needs to be silent, fast and accurate, because insects move so fast.

Nasty surprise

Crocodiles lurk just below the surface of a river. They spring out and catch an animal drinking at the water's edge. A crocodile cannot chew, so it swallows small prey whole. It uses its powerful jaws to bite and crush larger prey before it swallows them.

This chameleon is ready to strike. It stays very still, so the insect does not notice it. Only its eyes move.

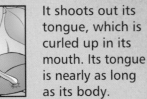
It shoots out its tongue, which is curled up in its mouth. Its tongue is nearly as long as its body.

The insect sticks to the tongue. It is pulled in and eaten.

This baby crocodile has caught a frog in its teeth. It will flip back its head and toss the frog into its mouth.

Frogs are one of a baby crocodile's favourite meals.

Special senses

Reptiles sense the world in the same way as other animals – with taste, smell, sight, hearing and touch. But some reptiles make use of these senses in unusual ways.

A tokay gecko uses its excellent hearing and night vision to help it find insects to eat.

A gecko has no eyelids. It uses its tongue to clean its eyes.

Night sight

Like many night hunters, the tokay gecko has big eyes to help it see every scrap of light. During the day its pupils close up to a little slit to protect its super-sensitive eyes from bright light.

The pupil goes very small during the day, and lets in very little light.

The pupil opens wide at night, to let in as much light as possible.

Snake table manners

Snakes have several fascinating and revolting ways of killing their food. Many can eat animals which are much bigger than themselves.

A snake can separate its upper and lower jaws. This lets it open its mouth very wide. Its body also stretches to hold the food it is eating.

The boomslang snake climbs trees and snatches birds from their nests.

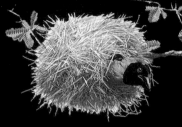

Like many snakes, the coral snake has poisonous fangs. These paralyse its prey.

This anaconda has squeezed a crocodile to death.

A flap of skin covers the back of the crocodile's throat, to stop it swallowing water when it dives.

You can see how the snake's jaws separate, so it can swallow this huge meal.

"Seeing" heat

Many reptiles have extra senses. A pit viper, for instance, can "see" heat. Two little pits either side of its head detect tiny amounts of heat given out by other animals' bodies. This extra sense lets it hunt in the dark.

The pit viper's pits are just in front of its eyes.

Cross-eyed

A chameleon's eyes can look in two directions at once. They swivel around in search of insects. No one knows if its brain sees one or two pictures at a time.

Notice how this chameleon's eyes are looking in different directions.

This eyelash viper is "tasting" the air with its tongue.

Forked tongue

Snakes have very poor eyesight and hearing. Most find their prey by smell and by feeling the vibrations through the ground caused by an animal's movements.

They also "taste" the air by flicking their tongue in and out. Doing this helps them to pick up the scent of other animals.

Reptile defences

Most reptiles must be constantly on guard to stay alive. Birds, mammals and other reptiles are waiting to snap them up in an instant. Here are some of the ways reptiles defend themselves.

This frilled lizard is trying to look frightening.

Getting bigger

Some reptiles make themselves look bigger and fiercer when cornered by an enemy. Most do this by spreading out part of their body.

This frilled lizard stretches out a frill of skin around its neck and steps forward, hissing loudly. If this doesn't work, it runs away.

Colour change

A chameleon can change the colour of its skin to blend with its surroundings. Its colour also shows its mood. Below, you can see how it changes colour.

The chameleon has gone bright green to match the leaves.

Now it has turned light brown to match the forest floor.

It goes stripy to warn an enemy when it is angry.

This chameleon is hiding in a tree.

Spikes

The moloch's body is covered with spikes as sharp as thorns. This makes it very unpleasant to chew.

This is a moloch. It is also called a thorny devil.

Tail trick

A special trick can often fool an attacker. Most lizards can break off their tail if attacked. The tail goes on wriggling for several minutes, distracting the attacker.

This skink lizard has shed its tail.

Playing dead

Many attackers only eat meat they have killed themselves. Some reptiles take advantage of this by pretending to be dead when threatened.

This ringed snake is pretending to be dead.

Young reptiles

Some reptile parents protect their eggs and their babies when they hatch. But most reptiles lay their eggs in a safe place and just leave the babies to fend for themselves.

Caring crocs

Nile crocodiles care for their babies. The mother lays 40 eggs, and both parents guard them for 90 days.

When the babies hatch, the mother gathers them in her mouth and takes them to a quiet pool to look after them.

This is a baby crocodile hatching from an egg.

A bad start

Turtles lay their eggs at night in burrows on the beach. The turtles then return to the sea. When the baby turtles hatch, they dash to the sea. The journey is very dangerous and many are eaten on the way by crabs and seabirds.

Baby turtles run as fast as they can, trying to reach the sea before they get eaten.

Here is a turtle laying her eggs in a burrow.

As it comes out of the egg, a baby crocodile makes little squeaking noises to attract its mother's attention.

Body nest

Snakes usually leave their eggs after laying them, but this python protects them by making a nest with her body. She lays about 100 eggs, and coils around them for about three months.

The eggs need to be warm to develop, so the python shivers to raise her temperature by a few degrees.

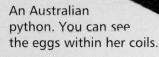

An Australian python. You can see the eggs within her coils.

Quick hatchers

Some reptiles give birth to live young, and others, such as the dwarf chameleon, lay eggs which hatch soon afterwards.

Many animals eat other animals' eggs. Staying in an egg for a short time gives a baby reptile a greater chance of surviving.

A chameleon lays a sticky egg on a twig.

The egg has a fully developed baby inside it.

After only a few hours, the baby hatches.

Miniature grown-ups

When reptiles hatch, they are fully developed and ready to face the world on their own. Although they are smaller than adults, they have all their parents' abilities and instincts.

A baby gecko, fresh from its egg

Creepy-crawlies

The world is full of tiny creatures. Over four-fifths of all known types of animal are creepy-crawlies. Here you can see some of the different kinds found within this miniature world.

Types of insect

A bee and a dragonfly are both insects. They behave very differently though. For example, bees live together in big groups, but dragonflies live alone.

The dragonfly (left) and bee (right) look very different, but they are both insects.

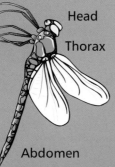

Head
Thorax
Abdomen

All adult insects have six legs and three parts to their bodies – a head, a thorax, and an abdomen. Most insects have wings at some stage of their lives.

Spiders

Spiders are not insects. They are a type of animal known as an arachnid. Spiders have eight legs and two parts to their body. They never have wings. Many spiders spin webs to catch their food.

The golden orb weaver is one of the biggest spiders in Australia. Females can be 45mm (2in) long.

Lots of legs

Millipedes and centipedes have the most legs of any animal. Their bodies are divided into a head and a series of segments. Centipedes have up to 100 legs, while some millipedes have up to 700. Like many creepy-crawlies, they have feelers on their heads called antennae.

Two rainforest millipedes mating

Slimy snails

Snails have a hard shell they can curl up in. This protects their bodies from enemies. Land snails, such as the one on the right, lurk in damp places, such as under leaves and stones. Some snails can live underwater.

Snails feed on plants. They scrape the surface with their rough tongue.

A snail can pull its whole body into its shell if it is attacked.

This is a kind of snail called a grove snail. Like all snails, it slides along on its slimy belly.

Baby bugs

Most female creepy-crawlies
lay eggs. Some leave their
eggs to hatch alone, others
guard them. A few even
look after their babies.

Parent care

Moths lay their eggs on leaves
and then fly off. The babies that
hatch are called caterpillars.
They come out of their eggs
with a huge appetite, but
have a good supply of food
all around them.

This moth
caterpillar
is eating a
leaf.

A wolf spider takes her eggs
wherever she goes. She spins a
cocoon to carry them, and looks
after them until they hatch.

A wolf spider carrying
her eggs in a cocoon

This female
scorpion guards
her eggs and then
carries her babies
around on
her back.

A scorpion
carrying
her
babies

46

Lookalikes

Some creepy-crawlies, such as snails and grasshoppers, have babies that look like small versions of themselves. A young snail's shell and skin grow as the snail grows.

Snail babies look just like miniature adults. Their shells grow as they get bigger.

A young grasshopper's skin does not grow. As the young animal gets bigger, a new, larger skin forms inside the old one. The old skin splits and the animal wriggles out.

You can see the old skin of the grasshopper's antennae.

This young grasshopper is wriggling out of its old skin.

The wings are still too small for the grasshopper to fly.

A big change

Some young creepy-crawlies look quite different from their parents. A ladybird's egg hatches into a grub called a larva. It grows, then makes a hard case around itself, called a pupa. Inside, it turns into an adult. After three weeks, the adult comes out. It is yellow but soon changes colour.

An adult ladybird laying eggs

Ladybird larva. It eats a lot and grows bigger.

Ladybird pupa. It is attached to a leaf.

New adult. It will soon turn black and red.

Bug food

Most creepy-crawlies eat only one kind of food. Many eat meat, but more than half feed on plants. Some even feed on the droppings of other animals. Here you can see some of the ways in which creepy-crawlies find, eat and store their food.

This ant has been stuffed full of honey by other ants in its colony. It stores the honey for when the colony is short of food.

Crickets have powerful jaws. They cause much damage to crops.

Mouth parts

An insect's mouth is designed to eat a certain kind of food. Below you can see three very different types of insect mouth parts.

A grasshopper has a pair of jaws which work like pliers. These nip off tiny pieces of plants.

A female mosquito has a long, sharp tube (shown here in red). She uses it to pierce skin and suck blood.

A fly has a mouth like a sponge to mop up its food.

Silky trap

Like many spiders, this orb spider spins a web to catch its food. The silky thread is made in a special pouch in the spider's abdomen.

This orb spider's web is sticky. Flies that land on it get stuck.

Web thread is made at the tip of the abdomen.

The spider's legs have an oily film on them, to stop them sticking to the web.

Dung

Dung beetles eat the droppings of other animals. The couple below are taking some back to their burrow. The female will lay eggs in it, so their babies will have a supply of food when they hatch.

Dung beetles

Suckers

Some insects, such as the assassin bug, inject spit into their victims. The spit dissolves the victim from the inside. The assassin bug then sucks the juices out.

This assassin bug is attacking a ladybird.

Colours and tricks

Creepy-crawlies come in all shapes and colours. Some have features which can trick or frighten an enemy. Others have their own built-in weapons.

Tail end

Real head

Invisible killer

A flower mantis is lurking on this bougainvillaea plant. Its shape and colour resemble the surrounding flowers. When another insect lands on the plant, the mantis pounces.

This butterfly has a false head on its tail end to confuse enemies.

To another insect, this flower mantis looks like a flower.

Watch it!

Some creepy-crawlies have alarming colours. The bright, shiny cases of these harlequin bugs can easily be seen against a leaf. The colours warn enemies that they taste nasty.

Enemies soon learn to leave these harlequin bugs alone.

Blob warfare

A sawfly larva feeds on pine needles, which contain a sticky liquid called resin. If the larva is attacked, it can also use the resin as a weapon.

A sawfly larva is attacked by an ant.

It coughs up a blob of sticky resin.

The larva gums up the ant with the resin.

Stings

Insects such as wasps and bees have a sting in their tail. This injects chemicals which hurt or kill an opponent.

This sand wasp is paralysing a caterpillar with its sting.

51

Butterflies

Butterflies are among the most colourful types of insect. Most live for only a few weeks. They mate, lay eggs, then die.

Butterfly wings

Butterfly wings are covered in tiny coloured and shiny scales. The shiny scales reflect light, which is why butterflies shimmer when they fly.

When a butterfly holds its wings open, as shown on the right, it is gathering warmth from the sun. This helps give it the energy to fly.

When it holds its wings closed, it is resting. It faces the sun, so the shadow it casts is small and enemies are less likely to spot it.

This butterfly is called a common blue. It has spread its wings to soak up the sun's heat.

Butterflies visit plants to feed. They drink nectar from flowers.

Butterfly with wings closed

Butterfly with wings open

Wing patterns

A butterfly's beautiful, patterned wings help other butterflies spot their own kind so they can meet and mate. Their wing patterns help butterflies in other ways, too.

A comma's ragged wings disguise it as a dead leaf when it is on the ground.

The circles on a peacock's wings look like eyes on a big face. This frightens enemies.

The African monarch is poisonous. Birds learn not to eat it.

An arctic ringlet's dark wings help it soak up heat in the cold area where it lives.

This mocker swallowtail is not poisonous, but birds think it is an African monarch and do not eat it.

The patterns on the tortoiseshell's wings help it attract a mate.

Making butterflies

A female butterfly lays her eggs on one particular plant. When an egg hatches, a caterpillar comes out and feeds on the plant. When the caterpillar is fully grown, it turns into a pupa, which has a hard case (see below). Inside the pupa, it changes into a butterfly.

A caterpillar ready to turn into a pupa.

The pupa forms inside the body. It splits the skin.

The pupa hardens. Inside, it is changing.

After two weeks a butterfly comes out.

The butterfly's body hardens and it flies off.

53

Living in the sea

The sea is full of life. Most sea creatures live around the coast, but you can also find them in the middle of the ocean, and on the deepest sea floor.

What is a fish?

All fish live in water. They have a skeleton inside their body, and most types are covered with small, smooth plates called scales.

Gristly fish

Sharks and rays are not like other fish. Their skeletons are made of gristle rather than bone, and they have rough scales.

This fish is a sweetlips. It has smooth scales on its body.

The scales on this ray feel like sandpaper.

Breathing

Fish "breathe" by pushing water over rows of feather-like gills at the back of their mouths. The gills take oxygen from the water.

The fish opens its mouth to take in water.

Water passes over gills and out of gill slit.

54

Other creatures

Not only fish live in the sea. From whales to starfish, there are as many different types of animal in the sea as there are on land. Here are some animals that all live by the shore.

A sunstar starfish uses its arms to grab other starfish and eat them.

Slugs

This brightly coloured sea slug is a relative of the much duller looking land slug. Its bright colours are a warning to other animals that it is poisonous.

This sea slug has stinging tentacles.

Shell home

Most crabs are protected by a hard case which covers their body. The hermit crab, though, only has a case over its front half. To protect the rest, it backs into an empty seashell and carries this around.

Hermit crabs find an empty seashell to protect their back parts. Here you can see the borrowed shell.

Worms

Many kinds of worms live in the shallows at the edge of the sea. This green leaf worm can be found crawling in rock pools and wet sandy beaches.

Green leaf worm

Baby fish

Most fish lay eggs. Some lay up to 200,000 at once. Many eggs will be eaten by other creatures, but some grow to be adults. Only a few fish look after their eggs before they hatch. Fewer still look after their young after they have hatched.

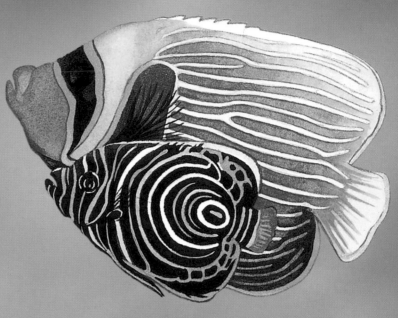

A young angelfish and an adult. The baby is a different colour so the adult will not think it is a rival, and attack it.

This male seahorse is carrying eggs in its swollen belly.

Seahorses

When seahorses breed, the male seahorse carries the female's eggs in a pouch in his belly. The babies look just like tiny adults, and they swim off as soon as they come out of the pouch.

Here you can see a baby seahorse coming out of its father's pouch.

Mouth cradle

A cardinal fish keeps its eggs safe by hiding them in its mouth. It doesn't feed while carrying the eggs, which may take up to a month to hatch. If it is disturbed or frightened, it may swallow all the eggs.

The eggs in the cardinal fish's mouth look like tiny glass balls.

Egg to fry

Most fish eggs float in the water, or lie among weeds or rocks. The young fish that hatch are called fry. Here is how an egg changes to a baby.

This fish egg is filled with yolk. The baby inside the egg grows by feeding on the yolk.

The baby has hatched. It still lives on the yolk which it carries in a sac under its body.

The yolk lasts until the young fish is big enough to find other food for itself.

Safe spot

After hatching, a baby fish is still in danger of being eaten by an enemy. A type of freshwater fish called a cichlid not only keeps its eggs in its mouth, it keeps its young there until they are big enough to hunt for themselves.

This cichlid is releasing her young from her mouth.

Sea hunters

Sea creatures eat what they can, when they can. Some may go without food for days. Others catch food all the time. Here are some of the ways they hunt.

Teeth and jaws

Gulper eel

These three fish have different-shaped mouths. A basking shark swims around with its mouth open. It catches tiny animals in its throat.

A gulper eel lives in deep water where food is scarce. Its huge mouth helps it eat fish of almost any size.

Basking shark

A barracuda has sharp teeth in its powerful mouth. It can take a bite out of a much bigger fish, then quickly swim away.

Barracuda

A fishing fish

An angler fish has a small, wriggling "bait" attached to its head. It lures other fish with it.

Octopus

This angler fish is lurking on the sea bed. It snaps up fish that come up to investigate.

Lots of arms

An octopus has eight arms which it uses to grab fish. It shovels them into a beak-like mouth on the underside of its body.

The octopus uses rows of suckers on its arms to grip its prey.

Lionfish

Fin trap

Lionfish use their long, spiny fins to steer small fish into the sides of the coral reef where they hunt. When the fish are cornered, the lionfish pounces.

Lionfish have very sharp, poisonous fins.

Sea monsters

The seas and oceans are patrolled by sharks – some of the fiercest hunters in the world. Creatures even more terrifying lurk within the depths of the ocean.

Rows of sharp teeth stick out of the shark's jaw.

Killing machines

Sharks have sharp, saw-edged teeth. These help them rip their food into pieces that are easy to swallow. The teeth often fall out, but new ones grow.

This sand tiger shark eats other fish. Three or four sand tigers will surround a group of fish and eat them all.

Cross section of a shark's lower jaw, showing teeth.

The shark loses a tooth when it bites a victim.

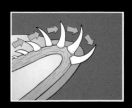

A new tooth moves forward to replace a lost one.

Dark life

The deep sea is a bleak place to live. It is dark and very cold, and no plants live there. The few fish that can survive here are very good hunters. They have to catch whatever food they can find.

This deep sea fish is called a pseudocopelus.

The teeth point back, making it difficult for other fish to wriggle free.

Teeth and spots

Most deep sea fish have a large mouth and very sharp teeth, to help them hold on to the food they grab. Many have luminous spots which act as a lure for other fish.

This viper fish has luminous spots on its body.

On and off

Flashlight fish have a luminous bulge just below their eyes. They can turn it on and off. Scientists think they may do this to signal to one another.

Tiny fish

This small lantern fish feeds on shrimps. It often swims up to the top layer of the ocean to hunt.

This lantern fish is no bigger than a man's thumb.

This flashlight fish has its light on.

Coral reefs

Coral reefs grow close to the coast in warm seas. They are full of fish and other sea animals. There is plenty of food here, and the reef has many caves and crevices to hide in.

Coral home

Reefs are made of tiny creatures called corals. Their soft bodies are protected by a hard outer skeleton. New corals grow on top of the dead skeletons of other corals. Millions of dead and living corals make up a reef.

Many different corals live side by side on the reef.

Inflatable fish

A fantastic number of different animals live on a coral reef. You can see some of them on this page. The creature below is a puffer fish. It blows itself up into a spiky ball if it is in danger.

A puffer fish usually looks like this.

When a puffer fish is in danger, it swells up. Its spikes make it unpleasant to eat.

Helping out

These blue and black cleaner fish are eating pests and dead skin on a big grouper fish. The cleaners get a free meal, and the grouper gets a good clean.

A small cleaner fish feeds quite safely inside a grouper's mouth.

Coral nibbler

Parrot fish get their name from the bird-like beak they have for a mouth. They use it to nibble the hard coral reef, and eat the tiny soft creatures inside.

Parrot fish

Bright colours

The creature on the right is a kind of sea slug. Its bright colours warn other animals that it is poisonous. The sea slug waves the flaps on the sides of its body to swim.

The orangey, finger-like structures are the sea slug's gills.

Index of animal names

Acknowledgements

Additional design: Jane Rigby
Digital illustrations: Richard Cox

Photo credits

Key. t - top, m - middle, b - bottom.

Bruce Coleman Collection: 4 (Erwin & Peggy Bauer), 24 (John Cancalosi), 25 (Dr. Scott Nielsen), 27 (Joe McDonald), 46 (Andrew Purcell), 47t (Waina Cheng Ward). **Corbis:** 7 (Jack Fields), 11 (Joe McDonald), 14 (Roger Wilmshurst; Frank Lane Picture Agency), 15 (Steve Kaufman), 18 (Karl Amman), 19 (Jean Hosking; Frank Lane Picture Agency), 22 (George Lepp), 23 (Wolfgang Kaehler), 30 (Wolfgang Kaeler), 32 (Uwe Walz), 33 (Johnathan Smith; Cordaiy Photo Library), 36-37 (Jonathan Blair), 39 (Kevin Schafer), 40 (David A. Northcott), 42 (Anthony Bannister; ABPL), 43t (Chris Mattison; Frank Lane Picture Agency), 43b (Michael & Patricia Fogden), 46 (Karen Tweedy-Holmes), 48 (Michael & Patricia Fogden), 49 (Anthony Bannister; ABPL), 50 (Michael & Patricia Fogden), 54 (Lawson Wood), 58 (Stephen Frink), 59t (Jeffrey L. Rotman), 59b (Stephen Frink), 62 (Lawson Wood), 63 (Robert Yin). ©**Digital Vision:** front cover (main picture), back cover, 1, 2-3, 17m, 47b. **Natural History Photographic Agency:** front cover t (Stephen Dalton). **OAR/National Undersea Research Program (NURP):** 55t. **Planet Earth Pictures:** 6 (K& K Ammann), 9 (Steve Bloom),10 (Ken Lucas), 12 (Anup Shah), 13 (Neil McIntyre), 16-17 (Frank Krahmer), 20-21 (Pete Atkinson), 21b (Doc White), 26-27 (Brian Kenney), 34t (Brian Kenney), 34b (K. Jayaram), 35 (S.J. Vincent), 44 (Geoff Du Feu), 45 (Mick Martin), 51 (David Maitland), 55b (Nancy Sefton), 56 (Georgette Douwma), 57t (P. Rowland), 57b (Georgette Douwma), 61 (Peter David). **Still Pictures:** 8 (M & C Denis-Huot), 29 (Michael Sewell), 60 (Jeffrey L. Rotman).

Every effort has been made to trace and acknowledge ownership of copyright. The publishers will be glad
to make suitable arrangements with any copyright holder whom it has not been possible to contact.

Illustrator credits

Sophie Allington, John Barber, Isabel Bowring, Trevor Boyer, Robert Gilmore, Rebecca Hardy, David Hurrell, Ian Jackson, Nicki Kemball, Steven Kirk, Rachel Lockwood, Malcolm McGregor, Dave Mead, Maurice Pledger, David Quinn, Chris Shields, Treve Tamblin, David Wright.